CHRONICLES OF FAITH

THE PILGRIM'S PROGRESS

John Bunyan
Retold by Dan Larsen

Illustrated by
Al Bohl

BARBOUR
PUBLISHING

ISBN 978-1-59789-966-6

Cover Illustration: Corey Godbey, Portland Studios, Inc.

Published by Barbour Publishing, Inc., P.O. Box 719, Uhrichsville, Ohio 44683, www.barbourbooks.com

Our mission is to publish and distribute inspirational products offering exceptional value and biblical encouragement to the masses.

ecpa Member of the Evangelical Christian Publishers Association

Printed in the United States of America.

CHRONICLES OF FAITH

THE PILGRIM'S PROGRESS

Introduction

Part One of John Bunyan's *The Pilgrim's Progress* was first published in 1678. Part Two followed six years later. This book has been read by more people than any other book except the Bible. It is among the greatest books on earth.

The Pilgrim's Progress is actually two stories. Part One is about Christian, who takes a long journey to the holy city. On the way he meets enough danger and adventure to turn any man back, but he must go on. Part Two tells the story of Christiana, Christian's wife. She, too, finds that she must make the same journey.

Here are tall mountains and dark valleys, great heroes and evil giants. Here, too, are ordinary men and women, who together face the perils of the pilgrim's journey.

This story is an allegory. That means that the names of certain people and places not only describe those people and places but also stand for something else more significant. Christian, for instance, is the story's hero. Yet his name also stands for every person who decides to follow Jesus Christ.

In that sense, this story is not make-believe. It is very real. Christian follows the same straight, narrow path through the wilderness that every Christian travels in his or her own journey through life.

And the end of the journey is just as magnificent in real life as it is in *The Pilgrim's Progress.*

PART ONE

"We are doomed!"

1

Christian Falls

The man stood in the field outside the City of Destruction and cried out in terror, "What shall I do?"

His clothes were ragged, and his back was bowed as if with a heavy load on his shoulders. He was reading a book, and what he read made him weep and tremble. His name was Christian.

That night at home, he tried to hide his anguish from his family but could not. He burst out, "We are doomed! I have learned that unless we escape this city we will all be burned by fire from heaven."

His wife and sons were astonished. "You have taken a fever," said his wife. "Go to bed now. Sleep will settle your wits."

But Christian could not sleep. He tossed and he turned. In the morning he said, "I am worse yet. And this burden is even heavier."

And this went on for many days.

Christian's friends, even his family, scorned him. "He has gone out of his mind!" they said.

So he spent his days alone, walking in the fields, reading his book, sometimes praying, sometimes weeping. One day as he stood reading, he cried, "What shall I do to be saved?"

Just as he said this, a man, tall and strong, walked up to him. "My name is Evangelist," said the man. "What troubles you so?"

"Oh, sir," said Christian. "I have read here that because of the bad things I have done I will die and be punished forever."

Evangelist then handed Christian a roll of paper. On it was written, "Fly from the wrath to come."*

"Which way?" cried Christian.

"Follow the light there," said Evangelist, pointing across a wide field. "You will come to a

*Matthew 3:7

“What shall I do to be saved?”

wicket gate. Knock at the gate, and you will be told what to do."

Christian saw the light shining far away, where the man pointed. Now he began running toward it. At last he felt some hope.

"Come back, fool!" came a cry from behind. Now two men from the city, whose names were Obstinate and Pliable, caught up with Christian and grabbed him by the arms.

"We saw you running away," they said. "We have come to bring you back."

"Never!" said Christian. "You live in the City of Destruction, which will be destroyed by fire. I go to find life."

And Christian told them of things promised in the book he had, of a life that lasts forever, a life free to all who flee the coming destruction.

"You have lost your wits, crazy fool!" said Obstinate, and he turned back.

But Pliable said, "If this life indeed be true, then I would seek it with you."

"We have come to bring you back."

And so they set out together.

As they walked, Christian read to Pliable from the book. "There is a kingdom that will last forever, and we will live forever in that kingdom, wearing crowns of glory and clothes that shine like the sun."*

The men grew eager for these things. And as their eagerness grew, they began to fear that something evil was following them and would catch them before they reached the kingdom. They began to run.

Suddenly they tumbled into a bog and began to sink. Pliable struggled desperately to the side and dragged himself out. "So! This is the life your Good Book promises," he snarled. "Well, not for me!" And he turned back to the city.

Christian sank deeper in the mire. The load on his back was dragging him under. Just as the bog closed over his head, he felt a strong hand grab his arm, and he was pulled out onto dry ground.

---

*Isaiah 45:17; John 10:27–29

A strong hand pulled him out.

Christian stood dripping filthy mud and looked into the kind face of his rescuer.

"My name is Help," said the man. "This bog is called the Slough of Despond. It is the dumping place of all the fears and doubts of people who are lost in sin. If you look hard, you will see steps through it that the King has placed here. But watch carefully!"

Christian did watch carefully then and crossed the bog safely. As he went on he met another man, Mr. Worldly Wiseman from the Town of Carnal.

"And where are you going, and why so bent over as if with a heavy load?" asked the man.

Christian told him of his journey and of the man, Evangelist, who sent him.

"Fah!" said Wiseman. "Evangelist! His is the hardest road to follow. Come, I will show you a way that is easy and where many pleasures await you."

Mr. Wiseman pointed to a high hill, where

"Watch your steps carefully!"

Mr. Legality lived in the City of Morality. "His is the first house you come to. He will ease that burden off you."

Christian eagerly set out for this hill. But as he started to climb, his burden grew heavier and heavier. Then suddenly flames shot out at him from the hill. He fell down in terror.

"Christian! Why have you come this way?" came a voice. There stood Evangelist, untouched by the flames as they lashed around him.

So Christian told him of Mr. Worldly Wiseman and Mr. Legality.

Evangelist said, "Listen to what the Lord says: 'Try to enter the narrow gate, because that way leads to life.'* All other ways lead to death. Mr. Legality only leads you away from the one place where you can leave your burden, which is your sins. That place is the Cross."

---

*Luke 13:24

Suddenly flames shot out at him.

He quickly pulled him through.

2

Christian Finds Grace

Christian repented for having turned out of the way. He felt ashamed for having taken Mr. Worldly Wiseman's advice. Now he went along, not speaking to anyone he met, until finally he reached the wicket gate. Over the gate was written, "Knock and the door will be opened to you."* So Christian knocked.

Soon a man came to the gate. "I am Goodwill," he said. "What do you wish here?"

"Sir," said Christian, "I came from the City of Destruction to escape the wrath that is coming, and I want to know if you are willing to let me in."

"With all my heart," said Goodwill.

But as Christian stepped up to the doorway, Goodwill quickly grabbed him and pulled him through. Goodwill pointed to a dark castle on a nearby mountain. "That is the castle of

*Matthew 7:8

Beelzebub," he said. "The evil beings there shoot arrows at those who try to enter here."

Now Goodwill asked Christian of his journey. Christian told him of the troubles he had met with on the way, of Pliable and how he had turned back, of Mr. Morality and the hill where Mr. Legality lived, and of the fire that stopped him from going farther.

"That hill has brought the death of many who turned aside," said Goodwill. "But happily you have escaped. Now look. There is your road," he said, pointing to a straight, narrow path. "There are many turnings, wide and crooked, but your way must always be on the straight and narrow."

"Go now," Goodwill said. "Soon you will come to the house of the Interpreter. He will help you understand many things about your journey here."

"Sir," said Christian, "I still carry this burden. Will you help me off with it?"

“There is your road.”

"You must carry that yet," said Goodwill, "until you come to the Cross."

Then Christian said good-bye to Goodwill and started on the narrow road. Soon he came to the house of the Interpreter and knocked on the door.

"Come in," said the Interpreter. "I will show you things that you will need to know."

The Interpreter lit a candle and led Christian into the parlor where the floor was covered with dust. A man came in and began to sweep. As he swept, the dust flew about the room so that Christian could hardly breathe.

"Now bring the water," said the Interpreter. A girl entered, sprinkled water about the room, then swept it clean.

"Now I will tell you what this means," said the Interpreter. "This parlor is the heart of a person lost in sin. The dust is his sin. The sweeper is the Law, which stirs up but cannot clean. The water is the gospel, which washes the heart clean."

The dust flew about the room.

Then the Interpreter brought Christian to a fireplace. A man stood there in a rage, throwing buckets of water on the fire. But with each dash of water, the fire only burned brighter.

Now the Interpreter took Christian behind the wall, where a man stood throwing fuel on the fire.

"What does all this mean?" asked Christian.

"This fire is the work of grace in a person's heart," said the Interpreter. "The man trying to quench the fire is the devil. The man fueling the fire is Christ, who always keeps alive every work He begins in a person's heart."

The Interpreter showed Christian many other things before he sent him on his way again. "Never let anyone lead you off the path," said the Interpreter. "Their way leads to death. And remember, the Comforter, God's own Spirit, will guide you through any hard places you come to on your journey."

But the fire only burned brighter.

Suddenly the load slid off his back.

3

Pathway to House Beautiful

Christian left the house of the Interpreter and started up the narrow road. His going was slow because of the load on his back.

Before long he came to a grassy hill. On it stood a wooden cross. Christian stopped. He stared in wonder at the cross. Suddenly, the heavy load on his back slid off and tumbled downhill. His burden was gone!

Christian felt so light! Tears filled his eyes as he thought of the One who had hung on that cross for him. "He has taken my heavy load by His sorrow," Christian said, weeping.

As he stood there, three men appeared. They shone like the sun.

"Peace to you," said the first. "Your sins are forgiven."

The second gave Christian new white clothing.

The third gave him a roll of paper. "This is

written for you," he said. "It will bring help to you when you are troubled."

Now the three men left Christian. He quickly took off his old, ragged clothes and put on the clean new ones. Then he gave a leap of joy and sang a song of praise to the One who had taken his burden.

He went on his way. On either side of the road was a wall called Salvation. Christian had not gone far when two men climbed over the wall onto the road just ahead. Their names were Formalist and Hypocrisy.

"Ho, there!" called Christian. "Where are you going?

"Why did you not come in at the gate?" he asked. "It is written, 'Anyone who does not enter by the gate but climbs in some other way is a thief and a robber!' "*

"Bah!" they said. "That way is much too hard. We chose an easier way."

*John 10:1

Christian gave a leap for joy.

"But won't the Lord of the City call you trespassers when you come there, if you were not invited in at the gate?" said Christian.

"You were invited," they sneered. "We climbed in. Now we are both here, and how are you better than we?"

"I am a guest here," said Christian. "You are trespassers."

They laughed at him at this. Christian went ahead on his way, and they followed. Now the road went up a steep hill called Difficulty. At the bottom was a spring. Christian drank deeply. Feeling refreshed, he started the long climb.

But the two men behind him turned away when they got to the hill. "Why bother with this long, hard climb?" they asked. "Let us find an easier way."

But as they went, they got separated. One wandered lost in a dark forest called Danger, the other in the Mountains of Destruction. They were never seen again.

Christian started the long climb.

The Hill of Difficulty was so steep that Christian had to climb on his hands and knees. About halfway up he came to a level spot with a shady bower set up for weary travelers. Exhausted, he lay down and fell asleep. The sun dropped in the sky, the day passed, and still he slept.

As he dreamed, a hand shook him and a voice said, "Sleepy one! Be wise, like the ant.* Awake!"

Christian, startled awake, climbed the rest of the way up the hill. Then he went on.

Suddenly he froze. From somewhere ahead came a scream of terror. Then two men, Timorous and Mistrust, burst past him and scrambled down the hill he had just climbed.

"Go back!" they cried. "Two huge beasts lie on the path before you! They will tear you to pieces!"

---

*Proverbs 6:6

"Go back!"

Trembling, Christian peered ahead in the growing darkness. What should he do now?

Suddenly Christian remembered the roll of paper the shining man had given him. "It will help you in your troubles," he had said. Christian reached for it. But it was gone!

Horrors! thought Christian. He must have dropped it on his climb. The only thing to do now was turn back. He slowly, painfully climbed down the hill. As he went he searched for the roll. "Oh, why did I sleep?" he moaned.

"Now I am done!"

At last he came to the bower, and there on the ground was the roll! Now he felt new strength. He began to climb again.

But by the time he reached the top, night had fallen. And the beasts lay ahead! Clutching his roll tightly, he walked on in the darkness. *The wild beasts hunt at night,* he thought. *This is the end of me!*

Just then a huge shape loomed out of the

The beasts lay ahead!

darkness. Terrified, Christian could only stare at it, waiting. Then he realized what it was. A castle. Maybe he could stay there for the night.

But as he went forward he saw just ahead, on either side of the road, two huge lions, still as statues. Christian turned to run. But a voice stopped him.

"Do not fear the lions! They are chained. They are there to turn back those who have no faith. Stay in the middle of the path, and you will not be harmed."

Christian crept past the lions as he was told. Though they roared terribly, they could not reach him. Soon he was past them. He came to the castle.

"I am Watchful, the porter," said the voice. "This house was built by the Lord of the hill. It is for the rest and safety of weary pilgrims. Welcome."

The porter brought Christian into the castle. There he met three sisters, Prudence, Piety, and

But the lions could not reach him.

Charity. They brought some food and sat down to eat with Christian.

As they ate they talked about his journey and of the people he had met. Then they talked of the Lord of the hill, the one who had built that castle. The Lord, said the sisters, had made princes of many poor pilgrims. And because of His great love, He had died on a cross for them. They talked late into the night.

Christian rested there for several days. When the time came for him to leave, the sisters brought him some weapons that the Lord had made: a sword, a shield, a helmet, a breastplate, a belt, and shoes that never wore out.

"They are for your protection against any evil you meet on your way," the sisters said. "Good-bye, Christian."

They gave him weapons.

A huge monster dropped out of the sky.

4

Through the Valley of Humiliation and Death

Now Christian's way went down into the Valley of Humiliation. He passed slowly through meadows and fields of lilies. Then suddenly the sun was blotted out for an instant.

Christian looked, just in time to see a huge monster drop out of the sky onto the road. The monster was covered with scales. He had wings like a dragon's, feet like a bear's, and a head like a lion's. He breathed fire and smoke.

"I am Apollyon," the beast said. "Where do you come from, and where are you going?"

"I come from the City of Destruction and am going to the City of Zion," said Christian, his voice trembling.

"You are from my country," said Apollyon. "I am the prince and god of that place. You are in my service. Do not go any farther. You must return."

"I serve another prince now, evil one," said Christian. "And I will not turn back!"

At this, a wicked light flared in Apollyon's eyes. He spread his wings. "You will die here!" he screamed.

He hurled fiery darts at Christian, one after another. Christian stopped the darts with his shield and drew his sword. He fought back with all his strength.

The battle lasted for hours. Christian was bloodied and weary. Finally he stumbled, and the sword flew out of his hand. In a flash, Apollyon was on him. But Christian grabbed his sword and thrust upward furiously—and his blade struck scaly flesh!

Apollyon screamed in pain. He flew off, spouting fire and blood. The battle was over.

Christian sank to the ground, praising the Lord. "In all these things we have complete victory through Him who loved us," he said.*

Now as he lay panting and bleeding, a hand appeared holding leaves from the Tree of Life.

*Romans 8:37

"You will die here!"

The hand touched his wounds. They were healed instantly.

Now as Christian went, he kept his sword in his hand. He crossed the valley with no more trouble.

But as night fell, he came to another valley. This was the Valley of the Shadow of Death. What Christian saw before him made a cold sweat break out on his forehead.

The road was very narrow here. On one side was a ditch that looked bottomless. On the other was a black, evil-smelling swamp. Here Christian's sword would do no good. He prayed aloud as he went forward.

Now from out of the pit came fire that licked across the path.

Now from out of the night came terrible voices. All around him they howled and screamed.

The voices, like demons from hell, came nearer and nearer. At last Christian cried, "I will walk in the strength of the Lord!" Suddenly the night was still. And Christian went on.

Fire licked across the path.

Christian looked back.

5

Christian Meets Faithful

Morning came. Christian had passed through the valley. Now he turned to look back. In the morning light he saw clearly the place he had gone through. "Only by the Lord's strength!" he said. "He has turned the shadow of death into the morning."*

The road now went up out of the valley. As Christian climbed he saw someone ahead of him. It was Faithful, a man from Christian's city. Christian called to him and ran to catch up with him.

The two went together, glad of each other's company on so lonely and difficult a journey.

"I would have followed you when you fled the city," said Faithful. "But you were too far ahead of me. So I came this way alone. Though everyone there was talking fearfully of the city's

*Amos 5:8

being burned, no one would come with me."

And Christian and Faithful talked of their journeys.

Faithful told Christian of the many people he had met, all of whom had tried to make him turn back. Some of their names he remembered: Deceit. Discontent. Shame. Pride. Arrogance. "What did you say to them?" asked Christian.

"That nothing they could say, no riches they could promise would make me go back," said Faithful, "because this is the path the Lord has set for me. I told them that a poor man who loves Christ is richer by far than the greatest man in the world who hates Him. And I told them that those who become fools for the kingdom of heaven are the wisest of all."

Soon they saw a man ahead of them. He was tall and from a distance looked handsome. But as they came up to him, Faithful saw something in his face that he did not like.

"Hello," said Faithful to the stranger. "Are you going to the heavenly country?"

They saw a tall man ahead of them.

"I am," said the man.

"Then let us go together," said Faithful.

"Very good. As we go, we can talk of good things. And what better things are there to talk of than God?"

"I begin to like you very much, friend," said Faithful.

As they talked, Faithful grew amazed at the man's knowledge of things good and evil.

But now Christian pulled Faithful aside. "Do you not know who this is?" he asked. "His name is Talkative. He comes from our own city. He speaks fine words and likes to appear a friend to everyone. But those who know him are afraid to turn their backs on him. He is full of lies and trickery. He preaches religion in his church, but among the drunken thieves at the alehouse he is the worst. Beware of him!"

Faithful was astonished at hearing this. "But he speaks truthfully of the Kingdom of Heaven, of the Good Book, and of the religion," he said.

“Beware of him!”

"His religion is on his tongue, not in his heart," said Christian. "People say of him, 'a saint abroad, and a devil at home.' Remember, saying is not the same thing as doing."

"I believe you, my friend," said Faithful. "I will test this man with a question."

So he said to Talkative, "Sir, tell me. What proof is there of a work of grace in a person's heart?"

"Great knowledge of the gospel," said Talkative proudly.

"But a person can have great knowledge and still no change in his soul," said Faithful. "You cannot please God with knowledge only. You must obey Him. Remember, the psalmist wrote, 'Teach me, Lord, the meaning of Your laws, and I will obey them at all times.' "*

Faithful went on. "Another proof of grace in the heart is the sorrow and shame that come on a person for the evil things he has done. And if a person leaves his sins at the Cross, the One who

*Psalm 119:33

“I will test this man with a question.”

died there and rose again will give him joy and peace in place of his sorrow.

"Have you done this, Talkative?" asked Faithful. "Can your religion stand this test?"

Talkative's face flushed. His eyes darted nervously. "Why are you asking me this?" he questioned.

"Because I have heard of you," said Faithful. "I know that outside you look clean, but inside you are full of dirt."

Talkative turned and stalked away. "You are not fit to talk to!" he snapped.

"His loss is no one's fault but his own," said Christian. "You did the best thing you could for him. You told him the truth."

He turned and stalked away.

"One of you must lose his life."

6

Vanity Fair

The road now led Christian and Faithful through a wilderness of forests and mountains. Here they met the one who had shown each of them the way to the gate, Evangelist.

"Welcome, my good friend," said Christian.

"A thousand welcomes," said Faithful.

"And how has it been with you since we last spoke?" asked Evangelist.

So they told him of all the dangers and hardships they had gone through.

"I am glad that you have been victorious in these things," said Evangelist. "Do not lose heart. A crown awaits each of you at the end of your journey here. Now you must hear what I have to say. Soon you will come to a town. You will be taken by enemies. There you must give testimony to the truth. One of you will lose your life for your faith. But that one will gain his reward in the eternal city sooner than the other."

Then Evangelist embraced them and left. They continued on their way in silence, each thinking about what Evangelist had told them.

Very soon they came to a town called Vanity. This town was built by Beelzebub and Apollyon. There were many things bought and sold there. And many evil men—thieves, murderers, swindlers—lived there.

As Christian and Faithful walked down the street they drew many stares. All along the street were carts of sellers loaded with everything imaginable. Many of the sellers jeered at the two men. Many more called out for them to buy something.

A fat, unshaven man spat at Faithful's foot and sneered. "What'll you buy, stranger?" he said.

"We buy only the truth," said Faithful.

The two friends met many more men like this. As the day went on, a crowd gathered

"What'll you buy, stranger?"

against them. "We must destroy these two," they whispered.

Christian and Faithful were grabbed and taken to the lord of the town.

"What do you mean, causing such trouble in our town?" demanded the lord. "Who are you, and what do you want here?"

"We are just passing through here, sir," said Faithful. "And there has been no trouble here of our making."

The lord could tell by the men's clothing and weapons that they were pilgrims. And he knew that pilgrims brought only trouble to his town. So he had them locked up in a cage and set in the street where everyone mocked them.

But Christian and Faithful kept quiet and did not return the insults to their tormentors.

Now, there were a few in that town not so bad as the rest. These began arguing with the others, saying they should let the men go. The argument became a fight, and soon the whole street was in chaos.

Christian and Faithful were grabbed.

Now the lord of the town was furious. He had the two men beaten and locked in irons. "You will die for this latest trouble you have caused!"

But they did not say a word.

The men were brought to trial. They were charged with being enemies to the town's trade of selling, and with causing a dangerous division among the men at the fair.

"These things are against the laws of our prince, Beelzebub," said the judge, whose name was Lord Hate-good.

Faithful answered, "We are men of peace and do not make trouble. Those men who came to our defense did so because they believed we were in truth and innocence. And as for your lord, Beelzebub, I defy him. He is the enemy of our Lord."

Three men from the fair, Envy, Superstition, and Pick-thank, took the stand and accused Faithful of many things.

“You will die for this!”

"This man is against all our customs," they said. "He has spoken evil of our lord and our town. He said that Christianity and our law stand against each other, that our religion is evil, and that our noble prince, Beelzebub, belongs in hell with other enemies of this man's God."

"Sirs," said Faithful, "I have said no wicked thing to anyone. I have spoken only the truth. The truth is, your laws are wrong if they stand against the Word of God. And anyone who follows your prince, Beelzebub, is himself an enemy of God."

For this, Faithful was condemned. He was dragged outside, whipped, and beaten until he died.

But just as the crowd of men were about to cheer at his death, they gasped. A chariot, drawn by two horses, rose up into the sky carrying Faithful.

"Blessed Faithful!" cried Christian. "Though they killed you, you are alive!"

The chariot rose into the sky.

An angel broke the cage door open.

7

Hopeful Joins Christian

After Faithful's death, Christian was locked in the cage again. There he awaited his own trial. But one night an angel came, broke the cage door open, and led Christian out of the town.

Christian gave thanks to the Lord and ran as far away as possible from that evil place. The next day he awoke and started on his way. He heard a cry from behind and turned to look.

A man came running up. "I am from Vanity," he said. "My name is now Hopeful; because of your friend's faith and yours, you gave me hope. I wish to go with you to the Celestial City. And there are many more like me in the town who, sooner or later, will take this road, too."

"My friend died for his faith," said Christian. "You have risen from his ashes and are now my companion. Welcome, friend."

They embraced and set out together.

About midday, Christian and Hopeful came to a small hill called Lucre. In that hill was a silver mine. In front of the mine stood a man who called to them.

"Ho, gentlemen," he said. "Come! I wish to show you something. In this mine is a treasure in silver. For a little digging, you can be rich men."

"Let us go see!" said Hopeful. He started to go.

"No!" said Christian, grabbing Hopeful. "I have heard of this place. Many have gone to this mine seeking treasure and have fallen into a pit, never to be heard of again. This man leads men to their deaths.

"Demas!" Christian called. "You are an enemy of the Lord's. Your father was Judas, the traitor, and you are no better than he. Be assured that when we come to the King, He will hear of you!"

And they left him.

"Come! I'll show you something."

Soon the two men came to a beautiful river. On the banks were soft meadows and many fruit trees. King David had called this place the River of God. John the Baptist called it the River of Living Water.

No evil could live in this place. The men rested there for several days, drinking from the river and eating fruit from the trees. When they were refreshed, they went on their way.

It was not long, though, before the road grew rough and rocky. They began wishing they had stayed by the river.

Soon the road went past a smooth meadow. Christian said, "Look. There is a path in this meadow that runs alongside the road. It would be much nicer to walk there."

So they crawled over the wall that ran alongside the road and went on in the meadow. Just then they saw a man walking ahead on the path.

Christian and Hopeful called to the man. "Sir, where does this path lead?" they asked.

They came to a beautiful river.

"To the Celestial City," he said. "I am Vain-confidence. Come. Follow me."

"Did I not tell you?" said Christian to Hopeful. "We are on the right path."

They followed the man for a few hours, until night fell. Soon it grew very dark. They lost sight of Vain-confidence.

Suddenly came a scream. Then all was silent. The two friends crept forward in terror.

"Stop!" cried Christian. In front of their feet gaped a dark pit. They could not see the bottom. "He must have fallen here," said Christian.

Now it began to rain. Then thunder boomed and lightning flashed.

"Oh, why did we go off the road?" cried Hopeful.

The men wandered in the storm, seeking shelter. At last they found a dry bank under a large rock. They crawled in and fell asleep.

That night Christian had evil dreams. He dreamed that he and Hopeful were lost at sea in

“Stop!”

a storm. The rain beat down on their heads, and the waves smashed them about.

He cried out in his sleep, "Forgive me, Lord, for turning out of the way! Do not let us drown here!"

Outside their rock shelter the rain pounded down and floodwaters rose. The men slept on.

"Awake!" came a terrible voice. Christian and Hopeful were jolted awake. Before them in the pouring rain stood a huge, grizzled giant.

"This is my land!" he bellowed. "No man comes here!"

The giant, whose name was Despair, drove them before him to his home called Doubting Castle. There he took them down a long flight of stone steps and threw them into a dank, foul-smelling dungeon. They heard a key turn in the rusty lock.

Then all was silent.

Many days went by as the two friends sat together in the dark dungeon. They grew weaker and weaker.

Before them stood a huge giant.

Suddenly one day the lock clicked, the heavy door swung open, and there stood the giant. In his hand was a massive club. He lurched into the room and viciously beat the men. Then he was gone, laughing.

Christian and Hopeful had never felt such despair! That night they prayed to God. They had prayed almost the whole night through when suddenly Christian jumped up.

"What a fool I am to have forgotten!" he said. "Look! I have a key called Promise that will open any door of Doubting Castle." Quickly he tried it in the lock. The door swung open!

The men climbed the stairs and ran to the outer door. It, too, opened to Christian's key. They were free!

They ran and ran until they came to the road again.

They were free!

"These mountains belong to the Lord."

8

The Shepherds and Delectable Mountains

After they escaped from Doubting Castle, the two friends were hungry, tired, and still sore from their beating. They went slowly along the narrow road.

Soon the road began climbing into some mountains. When the pilgrims reached the top of the first mountain, they found a beautiful land before them. Here were gardens, orchards, vineyards, and fountains of clear, sparkling water. The weary pilgrims ate and drank and rested.

As they walked about here, they came to a group of shepherds tending sheep. The pilgrims asked the shepherds what mountains these were.

"These are the Delectable Mountains," said one shepherd. "These, and the sheep on them, belong to the Lord. We are within sight of His city here."

Then the shepherds, whose names were Knowledge, Experience, Watchful, and Sincere, asked the men about themselves. And when the shepherds learned the men were travelers to the holy city, they said, "Welcome."

The shepherds invited Christian and Hopeful into their tents and shared their food and drink with them.

"You may stay here and rest from your travels," the shepherds said. "The Lord has made these mountains for travelers such as you. You may sleep in our tents tonight. Tomorrow we will show you some wonders in these mountains."

So the next day the shepherds took them to the top of a mountain named Caution. "Look down into that valley," said one shepherd.

The two friends looked and saw, far away, men wandering blindly among tombstones. The men seemed lost and sometimes stumbled over the tombstones.

"These men you see are ones who got off the

Men wandered blindly among the tombstones.

narrow road, thinking they found an easier way," said a shepherd. "They were caught by Giant Despair. That wicked giant put out their eyes and left them here to wander around forever."

After this the shepherds took Christian and Hopeful down a mountainside, deep into a dark ravine. On one side of the ravine was a blackened ancient door.

"Look inside," said a shepherd.

Cautiously Christian opened the door, and the two men peered inside. At first they could see nothing. But as they looked, they began to see a fire burning, faraway, deep under the mountain.

Then came a smell of bitter smoke.

Then came deep rumbling sounds.

Then came horrible cries of agony and terror.

The men shuddered as they quickly shut the door.

"This is a doorway to hell," said a shepherd. "There are many such doors. But this one is where liars and traitors enter. Here went Esau, who sold the birthright the Lord gave him. And

Cautiously they peered inside.

here went Judas, who sold the Son of God."

Christian and Hopeful looked at each other grimly.

The shepherds then brought the two friends to the top of another mountain called Clear.

One shepherd took a looking glass out of his cloak and handed it to Christian. "Here you can see the gates of the Celestial City—if your hand is steady enough to hold this looking glass."

Christian looked. He was still shaken by what he had seen and heard through that doorway. His hands trembled, and he could see nothing. He held on and gripped tighter. At last he caught a glimpse of a magnificent pair of gates. The sight was enough to ease his troubled heart.

Hopeful looked next, and he, too, thought he saw the gates.

Now the shepherds led them out of the mountains. As they said good-bye, one shepherd handed Christian a note. "Read this when you need instructions," he said. "And beware of the false one and of the Enchanted Ground."

"Here you can see the gates."

They carried a man bound with ropes.

9

Wayward Travelers Confront Christian

As Christian and Hopeful went down out of the Delectable Mountains, they sang for joy. They had seen the gates of the City! The end of the journey was near.

The going was easy for a little way. The road went past green meadows and forests.

Soon, though, it cut between two rugged cliffs. The pass was so narrow that the men had to walk one in front of the other. The cliffs blotted out all sunlight. The men went cautiously.

Christian stopped. "I hear something coming!" he whispered. Though they could not tell why, the two friends were afraid. They hid behind a large rock.

Suddenly down the path shuffled a group of tall, wiry-haired beasts carrying a bundle that struggled furiously. The beasts had long arms, wicked teeth, and horns on their heads. They carried a man bound with ropes. He writhed in their grasp and begged for mercy.

Now the beasts turned off the path. And Christian noticed a sign strapped to the man's back. It read *Apostate* (to turn away from faith in God). Then it seemed that the beasts disappeared right into the side of the cliff!

When Christian and Hopeful finally dared to come out, they crept to the place where the beasts had disappeared. There they saw a narrow cleft in the wall. They went to it and peered in.

This was another passage between two cliffs. Ahead on this path was the group of beasts. Then one of them opened a door in the cliff, and they all entered. The two men then recognized the door. It was the entrance to hell!

Christian and Hopeful got out of that dark place as fast as they could. As they went they prayed they would meet nothing else on that terrible path.

They disappeared right into the cliff!

Soon after the men were out of that passage, they came to a fork in the road. Both roads were up a hill. Neither was straighter than the other.

"Which way do we go?" cried Hopeful. "The roads look the same."

As they were talking about this, a man came to them. He was wearing a white robe with a hood. The two friends could not see his face.

"If you seek the way to the Celestial City, follow me," he said.

They gladly followed him. Their way went through a dense forest. As the road climbed, it gradually began to turn. The men did not notice this turning. They were busy picking their way through the briars and thorns that now reached out of the woods across the path. These grew thicker and thicker. Soon the men could go no farther.

Suddenly a net dropped over them. They were caught fast!

The figure in front of Christian and Hopeful

They were caught fast!

then threw off his robe. He was covered with black hair. He laughed through gleaming teeth, then disappeared into the dark woods.

The two men could barely move. They struggled with the net, but it was no use. "We have been tricked!" cried Christian. "Are we to die here now, so close to the end?"

Just then another man came up to them. He, too, wore a white robe. But His robe shone like the sun, and His face was fair. In His hand was a whip.

"Did the shepherds not warn you of the false one?" He asked. "The one who led you here disguised himself as an angel of light to deceive you. And did the shepherds not give you a note for your instructions? Why did you not read it when you came to the two roads?"

The shining one then slashed the net with His whip. It broke like a spider's web. And the two friends were free.

"Now I must punish you for following the

He laughed through gleaming teeth.

deceiver," said the shining One. "This will help you remember to follow the instructions you are given on your journey."

He gave each of the men a lash across the back with His whip. "Remember," He said, "I must sometimes punish those whom I love."

Then He led them out of those woods and showed them their road.

Though their backs stung from the whip, Christian and Hopeful felt such love for this Being that they wept. "Thank You for Your kindness in rescuing us, Lord," said Christian.

The shining One smiled at them. "Go now," He said. "And beware of evil counsel."

They started up the road. As they went they sang songs of praises to the Lord.

After they had gone some distance, Christian pointed ahead on the road. "Look," he said. "Who could this be, who is coming away from Zion?"

"Let us be careful of him!" said Hopeful.

He slashed the net with his whip.

"Remember that false one."

When the man reached them, he greeted them. "My name is Atheist," he said. "Where are you going?"

"To Mount Zion," said Christian.

At this, the man laughed in scorn. "To Mount Zion!" he said. "In all the world there is no such place. I once sought this city as you do now. I tell you, I have been seeking for twenty years. Twenty years I have wasted!"

"We have heard of and we believe in such a place," said Christian.

"Then look for it, fool!" laughed Atheist. "You will never find it."

"The Lord Himself put us on this path," said Christian. "So we walk by faith and not by sight."*

They turned away from the man named Atheist. He stood laughing at them as they walked away.

*2 Corinthians 5:7

"Let us be careful of him!"

Soon the road passed through a wide field full of flowers. As far as the men could see, there was nothing but flowers. They walked on and on. Their going became slower and slower. Their feet seemed to grow heavy. Hopeful yawned.

"Christian," he said. "I am so tired I can hardly hold my eyes open. Let us take some sleep here." He sank to the ground.

"No!" said Christian. "If we fall asleep here, we may never wake up!"

"What do you mean?" asked Hopeful, startled.

"Remember the shepherds' warning against the Enchanted Ground. This must be the place," said Christian. "This sleepiness is not natural. We must stay awake!" He helped Hopeful up.

"Let us talk to each other, to stay awake," said Christian. "Tell me how you came to have faith."

So Hopeful said, "In the town of Vanity, I lived like those others you saw at the fair. I loved the treasures of the world. As I bought them, I wanted them more and more. And I lived an evil life.

"We must stay awake!"

"But when you and Faithful came there, you appeared clean, where everyone else seemed filthy. And I heard Faithful say he bought only the truth. Then shame and sorrow began growing in my soul. I began to pray and to weep. But daily I grew worse. The things I once loved, I now hated. I hated even myself.

"Then Faithful said to me, 'Just believe in Jesus Christ, and He will set you free.' So I cried out to Him to forgive me. Then I wept, first in sorrow and then in joy."

As the two men talked of these things, their weariness washed away. And so they passed safely through the Enchanted Ground.

They passed safely through the Enchanted Ground.

“I would rather walk alone.”

10

Ignorance Ignores Christian

The two men had not gone far when they noticed a man behind them. They called to him, but he seemed not to hear. He came on slowly.

The men greeted him and asked him about himself.

"My name is Ignorance," the man said. "I come from a land called Conceit. I am going to the Celestial City."

"Then join us, friend," said Hopeful.

"I would rather walk alone," said Ignorance. "I will get to the city in my own time."

"How far have you come on your journey?" asked Christian.

"Not far," the other said. "My country is near the Delectable Mountains. I got on this road there."

"So you did not come in at the gate?"

"The gate! Everyone knows that is a long

way off. No, no. Why should I travel that far, just to return the same way?"

Christian and Hopeful looked at each other gravely.

Then Christian said to Ignorance, "But because you were not invited in at the wicket gate, you were not given anything to show at the gates to the city. Without some token to show that you are a guest here, you cannot be invited in."

"I think I can," said Ignorance. "I have lived a good life. I pray. I give money to the poor. The Lord will accept me for these things."

"You cannot gain entrance by the things you do," said Christian. "Your own righteousness (goodness and purity) will count for nothing at the gate. Only those who are made righteous by believing in the Son of God can enter."

"I know I am righteous," said Ignorance. "My own heart tells me so."

Christian said, "A wise man said, 'He who trusts his own heart is a fool.' "*

*Proverbs 28:26

"We're are not invited in at that gate."

"That was spoken of an evil heart," said Ignorance. "Mine is good."

"How do you know your heart is good?" asked Christian.

"Because it comforts me with hopes of heaven," said Ignorance.

"Your heart can deceive you. You may hope for things and yet have no reason for hope, because without Christ in your heart, you have no promise," said Christian.

"But isn't a good heart one that has good thoughts?" asked Ignorance. "And isn't a good life one that is in obedience to God's commandments?"

"Yes, indeed," said Christian. "But it is one thing to have goodness and another just to think you do."

"Why, what do you mean?" asked Ignorance.

"Your thoughts must agree with the Word of God," said Christian. "If they do not, they are not God's thoughts. And the Word of God says, 'No one, not anyone, is righteous.'*

"So if your thoughts tell you that you are

*Romans 3:10

"What do you mean?"

righteous, as you say, then your thoughts are not from God."

Ignorance seemed confused. "Then what would my thoughts be if they were from God?" he asked.

"Your thoughts would condemn you," said Christian, "because they would tell you the truth about yourself. And the truth is that, apart from Christ, you live in evil. As His Word says, 'Every imagination of the heart of man is only evil.'*

"Now, when your heart tells you that you are good, you are blinded to the truth about yourself," continued Christian. "And in that condition, you cannot enter the City of God."

"But you say I must believe in Christ," said Ignorance. "I do believe in Him."

"What do you believe in Him?" asked Christian.

"That He died for everyone and that He now accepts us if we obey Him," said Ignorance.

"This belief of yours is not found in the Word of God," said Christian.

*Genesis 6:5

Ignorance grew angry.

Ignorance grew angry. "What do you mean?" he said.

Christian explained. "This faith is not in Christ," he said, "but in yourself. True faith does not come from yourself but from God Himself. We cannot believe in Jesus as we wish to, but only as He really is. And He makes us acceptable to God by His own obedience, not by ours. He obeyed God His father and died on the cross. Now, no one can come to God except through Christ. And only God can reveal Christ in a person's heart."

Ignorance stood there, a frown on his face. Christian looked at him with love.

"Ignorance," he said, "if you ask God to show you His Son, Christ, He will. And Christ will show you your heart as it really is. And when He shows you the evil that lives in your heart, ask for His forgiveness, and He will give you a new heart. Then you can enter His city."

Christian looked at him with love.

“Welcome to Beulah Land.”

11

Crossing the River to the Celestial City

Christian and Hopeful now walked alone. Ignorance still would not go with them.

"You have your belief, and I have mine," he said. "You go on your way. I will come along as I wish." And he waited behind until they were out of sight.

"I pity this poor man," Christian said to Hopeful as they walked. "He will come all the way to the gates in his ignorance and not enter."

Soon Christian and Hopeful noticed that the land was changing. It was no longer harsh and desolate. Here were flowers and meadows and trees and birds. As the men walked they saw these things more and more. The sun, too, grew brighter and brighter.

Now they came to fruit trees, gardens, and vineyards. Here and there were openings in the wall by the road. These openings led into the gardens and orchards. In one of these gardens stood a gardener.

"Hello," he said. "Welcome to Beulah Land.

"These gardens are the King's," said the gardener. "They are for His delight and for any pilgrims who come here. Rest here if you wish."

Christian and Hopeful walked among the fruit trees and gardens, delighting in the beauty of the place. They found a vineyard of fat, juicy grapes, sweeter than any they had ever tasted. After eating their fill, they lay down and slept.

When they woke they felt fresh and strong. Just as they began to go on, two men in clothes that shone like pure gold met them.

"We have come to bring you to the city," the men said. "You are at the end of your journey. But before you can enter, you must face one more test."

"Will you go with us to help us?" asked Christian.

“We have come to bring you to the city.”

"We will go with you," they said. "But you must win through this test by your faith."

Now they all went on together until they came within sight of the city.

It was made of gold and precious jewels. It was so bright that Christian and Hopeful could not stare at it long. There in front of the city were two massive gates made of a single pearl.

But before the castle on the mountain was a deep, wide river. There was no bridge.

"How do we get across?" asked Christian.

"By your faith," said one of the men. "You will find the water as deep or as shallow as your faith is."

Christian went first. He took a few steps, then suddenly sank in up to his chin. "Help me!" he cried. "The water is going over my head!"

Hopeful stepped into the water. "Courage, Christian!" he said. "See? I stand on the bottom. You can, too."

But Christian floundered in the water.

"Help me!"

Hopeful reached out to him.

Hopeful struggled to keep his friend's head out of the water.

"I am being punished for my sins," gasped Christian. "The Lord wishes to drown me here so I will not enter His city."

"Christian!" said Hopeful. "This is not punishment! It is the test the shining one spoke of."

Suddenly Christian remembered. The test! "Give me faith, Lord!" he cried. Then suddenly his feet found the bottom.

Soon he and Hopeful stood on the other side of the river.

Then the two friends started up the long hill toward the city. As they went, crowds of people came down, laughing, singing, and dancing, to meet them and walk with them. Now Christian and Hopeful sang, too.

And all the people and all their praises went up the holy mountain into the clouds and into the City of Heaven.

Part Two

Christiana grew troubled.

1

Christiana Follows Christian

In the City of Destruction there was great talk. The people there had heard rumors and reports of Christian's journey to the Celestial City. They heard of his battle with the winged terror Apollyon, of his being captured by the giant Despair, and of his going through the Valley of the Shadow of Death.

And, last, they heard of his entering the City of Heaven. Some in the City of Destruction still called Christian a fool. But many more now called him a hero. A few secretly wished that they, too, were brave enough to go on such a pilgrimage.

Christian's wife, Christiana, grew more and more troubled. She missed her husband so! And she remembered how terrible she had treated him in his anguish. His cry "What must I do to be saved?" still rang in her ears. He had begged her to go with him. And she had scorned him!

One day Christiana burst into tears. "Oh, why did I not believe him!" she cried. "I could have gone with him. Because I sinned, he is gone from us forever!"

Her four sons heard her, and they wept, too.

That night Christiana had a dream. First, she dreamed a roll of paper came down from heaven and opened to her. In it was written every bad thing she had done in her life. She cried out, "Lord, forgive me! I have sinned!"

Then she dreamed that two evil-looking men stood by her bed. "What shall we do with her?" one said. "If she goes on like this, we will lose her just as we lost her husband." The other hissed through his teeth, like a snake.

Christiana woke in a cold sweat. She got on her knees and prayed. Then she woke her sons. "Come!" she said. "We must leave."

Soon a knock came at the door. A man entered.

"What shall we do with her?"

"Peace to this house," he said. "I am Secret. I live with those in the house of the Lord. I have been sent to give you this." He handed her a letter written in letters of gold. "It is the King's invitation to His palace," said Secret. "Keep it with you. You must give it at the gates of the city when you come there. Your journey begins at the wicket gate, as did your husband's."

There was great excitement in Christiana's house. Quickly she and her sons prepared to leave.

Later that day two neighbors, Mrs. Timorous and Mercy, stopped to visit.

"Where are you off to?" asked Mrs. Timorous.

"We are going to where my husband, Christian, has gone," said Christiana.

"Oh, what madness!" said Mrs. Timorous. "First your husband, and now you!"

But Mercy was silent.

Christiana told her visitors of her dream and of her special visitor. She showed them her invitation from the King.

"It is the King's invitation."

Mrs. Timorous only sneered. "Come, Mercy," she said. "Let us leave fools to themselves. We have better things to do than visit with the likes of her."

But Mercy stood still. "I think I will go a little way with Christiana," she said. "I wish to see her off on her journey."

"I see you are taken with silliness, too," snapped Mrs. Timorous. "Well, let fools go where they will, I always say." She hurried away.

Then Christiana, her four sons, and Mercy set out across the fields toward the wicket gate. Christiana was glad for Mercy's company. The two talked in the warm sunshine as they went.

Mrs. Timorous scurried around to all her friends' houses to spread this last bit of gossip. "Oh!" she said. "You will never guess what has just happened. . . ."

They set out across the fields.

“Come with us!”

2

Mercy Goes with Christiana

As the two women walked, Mercy seemed to grow troubled.

"What is wrong?" asked Christiana.

"My heart is sad," said Mercy. "Soon I must leave you and go back. I wish I would never have to see that city again."

"Then come with us!" said Christiana. "I would dearly love to have your company."

"But I cannot," said Mercy. She began to weep. "You have an invitation from the King. He has not invited me. Perhaps I am not wanted there."

"You may come at my invitation. I do not believe the King would turn away anyone who desires to come to Him."

"But I do not have the hope that you do."

"Go at least to the wicket gate with us," said Christiana. "It will not take us long to get there. And when we come to the gate, I will plead with the gatekeeper for you." And Mercy agreed to this.

As they walked, Christiana suddenly said, "Stop!"

Just ahead lay the swampy ground where her husband had fallen, the Slough of Despond. Pliable, who had also fallen in with Christian, had told all the town of that place.

"Look," said Mercy. "There are steps through it. Let us go carefully."

One after another, they made it across. The rest of the day went well. They met no trouble. Now they were at the wicket gate.

Christiana knocked. There was no answer. She knocked again, harder. Still no answer. They stood wondering what to do, when suddenly behind them came the barking of what sounded like a giant dog. Terrified, Christiana knocked again, harder and harder.

"Who is there?" came a voice. At the sound of the voice, the barking stopped.

Terrified, she knocked again.

"I am Christiana," she said. "We have come to take the road my husband traveled. May we enter?"

The gate opened. "Come in, wife of Christian," said the keeper. "And you," He said to the boys, "you children are always welcome here."

Christiana and the boys went in. The gate shut. And Mercy was left outside!

"Oh!" she cried. "I cannot enter! Now I will be torn to pieces by that dog!" And she fainted.

Inside, Christiana said, "My Lord, I have a friend outside who wishes to go with me to the City of the King. She fears she cannot come in here because she was not invited."

The keeper opened the gate and saw Mercy lying on the ground. Quickly He took her hand and helped her up.

"Oh, Lord," she said. "I was not invited. But I ask You to have pity on me, too, and let me in."

"I give life to all who believe in Me," He said, smiling. And He led her in through the gate.

Mercy was left outside!

Then the keeper asked Christiana, "Why did you knock so hard?"

"We were afraid to be left outside," she said. "And I believed that our only hope was to get in through the gate."

"Your faith has opened the door," said the keeper. "That dog you heard was sent by an evil one to frighten away pilgrims. Many have heard him bark and have fled this gate."

Then the keeper showed them their road, and they started out.

They had not gone far when two men jumped over the wall by the roadside. Christiana gasped! They were the men she had seen in her dream.

Just as they were about to grab her, a voice said, "Stop!" They turned and ran.

The voice belonged to a tall soldier. "I am of the house of the keeper," he said. "Do not fear. Soon the Lord will send a guide to protect you on your journey."

"Stop!"

The raker would not take the crown.

3

The Interpreter's House

Christiana, her sons, and Mercy next came to the same place where Christian had stopped, the house of the Interpreter. Here they knocked and were invited in.

"We of this house are very glad you have come, Christiana," said the Interpreter. "We have already heard of your starting on this journey. The Lord's messengers travel fast. Now come. While our dinner is being prepared, let me show you some things."

And he took them into the same rooms he had showed Christian and explained everything to them. Then he took them to some other rooms.

In the first of these a man was raking a pile of straw and dirt. Before him stood another man who held out a crown. But the raker would not take the crown.

"The riches of the world are like straw and dirt," said the Interpreter. "This man would rather have them than an eternal crown."

Then the Interpreter took them into the best room in the house. It was very beautiful. But on one wall sat a poisonous spider.

"Tell me what you see here," said the Interpreter.

They all looked around the room.

"I see nothing special," said Mercy.

"Look again," he said.

"I see a spider on the wall," she said.

"Is there just one spider here?" he asked.

Christiana began to weep. "Sir," she said, "there are two. And one of the spiders is much more poisonous than the other. I was like a poisonous spider when I scorned my husband for his faith. With my sharp tongue, my bite was more deadly than that spider's."

The Interpreter smiled. "And yet," he said, "like this spider, the person who is full of his

On the wall sat a poisonous spider.

poison of sin may yet come to repent and live in the very best room in the King's palace."

Now the Interpreter led the group outside and into his garden. There on the grass hopped a little robin. In its mouth was a great black spider.

"This robin is like many people who pretend to be Christians," said the Interpreter. "They, like this robin, are nice to look at and are thought well of by other people. In the streets and the churches they appear blameless. But at home, when no one is watching, they greedily gobble down sin like poison."

Soon dinner was ready. A table laden with all kinds of meats, fruits, and pastries was set up in the garden under the branches of sweet-smelling lilac trees. The Interpreter called his minstrels, and they came and played and sang and danced.

Christiana, her sons, Mercy, and all the people of the house ate and talked and laughed together under the stars, long into the night.

A table was set up in the garden.

Christiana and Mercy woke with the sun the next morning. They went out into the garden, where they met a lady of the house.

"A bath has been prepared for you," said the lady. "Before you leave, you must first wash from yourselves the soil of that country beyond the wicket gate."

After they had bathed they were brought new, white linen gowns. The boys, too, were bathed and given new clothes.

Then the Interpreter came into the garden. He lightly drew a mark on the two women's foreheads.

"This is the King's mark," he said. "Now you will be known as His wherever you are."

Then the Interpreter called, and out of the house came a tall, strong man. At his side hung a great sword. On his bearded face were faded battle scars.

"I am Great-heart," he said, bowing low. "I will take you to the House Beautiful."

"I am Great-heart."

Everyone knelt and worshipped.

4

Great-heart Guides Christiana

With Great-heart leading them, the group now set out on the narrow road. Soon they came to the cross on the hill, where Christian's burden had fallen off.

Here they stopped. They all stared at the cross. As they stood there, tears came to their eyes. Everyone knelt and worshipped.

"The One who died here carried our sins on His own shoulders," said Great-heart. "He obeyed God and came here to be punished for us. And with His blood He washes us clean, we who will believe in Him. It is by His death that you are able to go on this journey to His city."

"So it was this that made Christian's burden fall off here!" said Christiana. "Now that I am here, I, too, feel as though a great weight has been lifted off me."

"No one ever need carry his burden past this

cross," said Great-heart.

After they had worshipped a little longer, they started out again. The road went down the hill from the cross and then started to climb again.

Just before this hill, by the side of the road, three men hung from their arms and legs in iron collars. They stared in misery at the pilgrims.

"Who are these men, and why do they hang here?" asked Mercy.

"Their names are Simple, Sloth, and Presumption," said Great-heart. "For years they have lain here by the road and called out to pilgrims as they passed. 'Leave the road,' they would say, 'and eat and drink with us. Enjoy yourselves. There is no need for you to walk this hard road.'

"They said many evil things about the Lord, as well," continued Great-heart. "With their lies they have turned away many pilgrims on this road. These men hang here now in punishment for their wicked deeds."

“They hang here in punishment.”

Just a little past the three men, at the bottom of the hill, ran a stream. The travelers were thirsty and went to the stream for a drink. But the water was too muddy to drink.

"This stream is where Christian quenched his thirst before climbing the Hill of Difficulty here," said Great-heart. "It was once clean and good. But evil beings have come in over the wall to tramp in the waters and muddy it with their feet. They do this simply because they hate all pilgrims to the Celestial City."

"Can we do nothing to quench our thirst?" asked Christiana.

"Yes," said Great-heart. "Put some water in a clean vessel. The mud will settle to the bottom, and the water will be clean again."

So they did this. After a little while, when the mud had settled, they all drank some water. Refreshed, they started up a long climb.

At the top of the hill Great-heart told the group of the lions ahead. "But do not fear

They started up the long climb.

them," he said. "They are chained."

And soon they came to the lions. But the lions were not alone. Behind them on the road stood a giant. His huge arms were smeared with dried, blackened blood.

"If you come any farther I will kill you!" he roared.

Everyone stared in horror. Everyone except Great-heart. Out flashed his great sword.

"You stand in the King's highway!" he thundered. "I am the King's champion. Your days of murdering pilgrims are over!"

The giant roared in laughter.

But the laughter soon died in his throat. Never had he faced such a foe!

Great-heart came on. His sword blade a flash of whistling fury, he chopped at the giant. Again and again and again.

Finally, like an oak tree crashing to the ground, down came the giant.

Out flashed his great sword.

The lions roared and lurched against their chains.

5

At the Palace

Great-heart led the frightened pilgrims past the lions. The lions roared and lurched against their chains. Christiana and Mercy shuddered as they walked past the dead giant.

Soon it would be dark. Ahead lay the House Beautiful. "We must hurry," said Great-heart. "It is not good to be out here after dark."

When they came to the house, Great-heart called out. The porter inside knew Great-heart's voice because the warrior had many times led pilgrims this way.

"Come in," said the porter. "Welcome."

"This is Christiana," said Great-heart, "the wife of Christian, who stayed here before. She and her people here are going to the Celestial City." Great-heart turned to go.

"Wait!" cried Christiana. "Please do not leave us!"

"I must return tonight," he said. "You did not

ask my Lord for a guide, so He cannot send me farther. Yet, you may still ask Him this. And I will return."

"Christiana, wife of Christian," said the porter, "we have been expecting you. Your husband stayed here on his journey. You are among friends here. Now come. Dinner is waiting."

They all sat down to a delicious meal of roast lamb. They ate and ate. Then the pilgrims were shown to their sleeping rooms.

Mercy and Christiana shared a room. They lay awake a little while, talking excitedly about their journey. From somewhere in the house came soft music that fell on their ears like raindrops of joy.

In the morning Christiana said, "Mercy, why were you laughing last night?"

"I must have laughed in my dreams," said Mercy. "I dreamed I was alone in darkness and voices were laughing at me. I was weeping. Then a bright being came, wiped my tears, and led me to a golden palace. Inside sat the King

“We’ve been expecting you.”

on His throne. 'Welcome, daughter,' He said."

Christiana and Mercy went downstairs to breakfast. Three girls of the house, Prudence, Piety, and Charity, ate with them.

"Please stay here with us for as long as you like," said Prudence. "We love having you here."

So they stayed there for many days. They grew to love the people of the house. They spent their time walking about the grounds outside or sitting indoors, talking and laughing with one another. Christiana, Mercy, and the boys learned much of the wisdom of God from Prudence, Piety, and Charity.

One night Mercy and Christiana lay awake talking. A soothing breeze danced in through their open window. Mercy stared out at the stars glittering in the summer sky.

"I love this house," she said dreamily. "I wish we could stay here forever."

"The Lord is so good to us," said Christiana. "Just think! Someday I will see my dear husband again in paradise."

"I love this house."

One day Christiana's oldest son, Matthew, became very ill.

"Call Mr. Skill," said Prudence.

"Who is this Mr. Skill?" asked Christiana.

"He is the good doctor," said Prudence, "one of the King's subjects. He has helped people for as long as anyone can remember. No one knows how old he is."

Soon the doctor came and examined Matthew. "Something poisonous lies within," he said. "What has he eaten?"

"Nothing but the food of this house," said Christiana.

"Wait," said another son Samuel. "Just inside the wicket gate an apple tree hung over the wall onto the road. Matthew ate an apple."

"Ah," said the doctor. "That tree belongs to the evil Beelzebub. It hangs over the wall to tempt pilgrims. Its fruit is deadly."

He gave Matthew a drink of something. Matthew fell asleep.

"This medicine will cleanse your son as he sleeps," said Mr. Skill.

The doctor gave Matthew a drink.

The doctor made some of this medicine into pills. He gave them to Christiana to take along on their journey.

"This is mixed with tears of repentance," he said. "It will cure any disease that pilgrims may fall into."

Soon the day came when the travelers began preparing to leave.

Then Christiana remembered. Great-heart! They could not go without him. Quickly she wrote a letter asking the Interpreter to send his guide. The porter of House Beautiful sent a messenger with the letter.

In a few days Great-heart arrived. "My lord, the Interpreter, sends each of you this bottle of wine and this bread," he said to Christiana and Mercy. "And to you boys, these figs and raisins. They will refresh you on your journey."

Prudence, Piety, and Charity and the porter all walked with the travelers down to the road. Everyone embraced and said good-bye. Then the pilgrims set out.

The pilgrims set out.

The way down was very steep.

6

Trials in the Valley of Humiliation

The road down into the Valley of Humiliation was very steep. Everyone went down carefully. At the bottom the land opened out into softly rolling hills.

"We need not be afraid of this valley," said Great-heart. "Here the humble may walk in peace. Only those who think highly of themselves find danger here. The Word says, 'God resists the proud but gives grace to the humble.' "*

The travelers did not hurry here. They walked through green meadows and fields of lilies. Butterflies flitted about, and the songs of birds filled the air.

"Our Lord used to love to come here," said Great-heart. "He loved to walk these meadows and breathe this sweet air. And here men have

*James 4:6

met angels and found pearls. There is none of the noise and troubles and confusions of life here. Only peace and beauty. No one walks here but those who love to walk a pilgrim's life."

Soon they came to a small, flat, grassy plain.

"This place is called Forgetful Green," said Great-heart. "Here is where Christian had his battle with the winged beast Apollyon. There is still some of Christian's blood that can be seen on the stones here. And a few broken darts from Apollyon still lie shattered in the grass.

"Your father fought a great battle here," he said to the boys. "Hercules himself could have done no better against Apollyon. Come, let me show you something."

Great-heart led the group a little past the plain. There stood a stone monument. Great-heart read the words carved on it:

Here was a battle fought, most strange and yet most true.
Christian and Apollyon sought each other to subdue.
The man so bravely played the man,
he made the fiend to fly.

There stood a stone monument.

Of which a monument I stand, the same to testify.

After this, the road went down again. The land became rock-strewn and barren. There were no sounds of birds.

"We are coming to the Valley of the Shadow of Death," said Great-heart. "Follow right behind me and stay close together."

As they went forward they began to hear voices in the air. The voices were moaning and screaming. They grew louder and louder. The women's faces were pale. The boys were shivering.

"Have courage!" said Great-heart. "But watch your steps carefully. There are snares here."

Suddenly the ground began moving under their feet.

"Quickly!" shouted Great-heart. They leaped forward. The ground collapsed behind them.

Then began a hissing in the air, like a great serpent.

Christiana gasped. "Look!" she screamed. "Something is coming toward us on the road! I have never seen such a shape!"

"Something is coming!"

"Stay behind me!" said Great-heart. He whipped out his sword. "I will meet this fiend."

Great-heart strode down the path toward the thing. It kept coming. Closer and closer. Now it was towering over Great-heart. But he never stopped.

Then the thing spread out two vast wings. Great-heart raised his sword.

And the thing vanished!

Great-heart came back to the group. "You see?" he said. " 'Resist the devil, and he will flee from you.'* Let us go forward."

"Thank the Lord for such a brave guide!" said Christiana.

Suddenly Mercy screamed. "Behind us!" she cried. "A great lion is stalking us!"

A deafening roar shook the ground.

Great-heart took to the rear of the group. The lion charged! And Great-heart went to meet it head-on.

Now the lion slowed its charge then stopped. Great-heart kept coming!

*James 4:7

The lion charged!

Suddenly the lion turned and loped off down the path.

Great-heart took his place in front again and led the group onward. "Just a little farther," he said.

They had not gone far when suddenly a black mist settled over them. They were covered in inky darkness.

"Do not fear!" said Great-heart. "Stand still, everyone. We will win through this, too."

Suddenly the hairs on the back of Christiana's neck stood on end. She opened her mouth to scream, but no sound came out. From out of the writhing mist, a cold hand had touched her face!

Now she and the rest of the group heard and felt the air moving around them. Things flitted past them in the darkness. Hollow voices moaned and howled among them.

Then Great-heart's voice boomed out, "Lord, let Your light shine on our darkness!"

And light came.

Like lightning from heaven, it flashed to the

Like lightning, light split the darkness.

earth. It split the darkness with a crackle.

And in that light that was brighter than sunlight, the travelers went on through the valley.

The travelers were almost out of the valley when they came to a cave by the road.

"Great-heart!" came a huge voice from inside the cave.

Everyone stopped. Out of the cave stepped a giant. His name was Maul. "Great-heart," he said. "This is your last journey! You have robbed the prince of this world of too many people. And this group with you will never see the City of Light."

"I am the King's servant," said Great-heart. "He has commanded me to guide His people from the darkness to the light. Do not oppose me! I come against you with the strength of the Lord."

The giant lumbered toward Great-heart, swinging a massive club. Great-heart drew his sword.

But the giant was quick! His club smashed down onto Great-heart's head. Great-heart

Great-heart dropped to his knees.

was breathing hard. Blood was running down his face. He knelt and prayed for strength.

The giant was rested. "Now you die!" he said, swinging his club.

But Great-heart, ducking a savage blow, drove his blade clear through the giant. As the giant sank to his knees, Great-heart swiped off his head.

Then everyone shouted and laughed and clapped one another on the back.

“Now you die!”

"You should not be out here when darkness comes."

7

Gaius Welcomes the Pilgrims

It was growing dark when the band of pilgrims came out of the valley. As the road climbed, the land grew friendlier. Here and there were trees, and here grass grew again.

They came to an old man sleeping under a tall oak tree. They knew he was a pilgrim by his clothes and his staff.

Gently Great-heart woke him. "You should not be lying out here when darkness comes," he said.

"I must have fallen asleep," the man said. "I was so tired I lay down here. I have come on a hard journey."

"Come with us," said Great-heart. "These are pilgrims, too. We would welcome your company.

"This is Christiana," said Great-heart, "the wife of Christian who came this way before.

These are her sons, and this is her friend."

The man's eyes went wide. "Christian's wife!" he said. "Christian's name is spoken all through these parts!

"My name is Honest," the man continued. "I would be honored to join your company."

They set out together. They walked for hours in darkness. The women and the boys grew weary.

"Just ahead is an inn," said Honest. "The owner is a good man. His name is Gaius. I know him well. He will let us stay with him tonight."

When they got to the inn, all was dark. Honest knocked. Soon a lantern shone in the window. "Who is there?" came a voice from inside.

"It is your friend, Honest," he said. "My friends and I need a place to stay tonight."

They were welcomed inside and given rooms. The exhausted pilgrims immediately fell asleep.

But Great-heart and old Honest sat up with Gaius all through the night, sharing what news they had and talking of the Kingdom of

A lantern shone in the window.

At breakfast the next morning Gaius said, "Mr. Great-heart, I have heard much of your great strength and fierceness in battle. You are truly the King's champion.

"There is one thing I wish to ask you," continued Gaius. "Not far from here lives a giant. He is called Slay-good. He has killed many of the Lord's pilgrims. No one can come against him. We of this land would be forever grateful if you could rid us of him."

"Take me to him!" said Great-heart. He buckled on his sword.

Gaius brought Great-heart to the giant's cave. The giant clutched a man in his fist. The man whimpered as the giant poked at him, feeling his ribs.

"Giant!" said Great-heart. "Now you will pay for murdering the King's subjects!"

The giant dropped the man and reached out with long arms to crush this new enemy. But soon the giant lay dead on the ground.

The giant reached out to crush him.

Now Great-heart went up to the man he had saved from the giant. "Who are you, and how did this giant capture you?" he asked.

"My name is Feeble-mind," said the man. He was pale and very skinny. "I have been very sick. I decided to go to the Celestial City. Weak that I am, I thought that if I could not run I could walk, and if I could not walk I would crawl. But as I was going this giant caught me. He was trying to fatten me up before he ate me."

"Come to my inn," said Gaius. "I welcome all pilgrims. Stay as long as you like."

So Feeble-mind went with them.

Soon after, a man on crutches came to the inn. He, too, was a pilgrim. But his journey was a long one because of his crutches. He and Feeble-mind became good friends over the days that followed.

After many days had passed, the pilgrims set out. They said good-bye to Gaius, thanking him for his kindness.

"My name is Feeble-mind."

But Feeble-mind hung back. "You go ahead of me," he said. "I cannot go as quickly as you, and I do not wish to be a burden to you."

"My brother," said Great-heart, "my duty is to comfort the feeble-minded and to support the weak. I will not leave you behind."

The crippled man, Mr. Ready-to-halt, came up to Feeble-mind. "Take one of my crutches if you wish," he said. "I do not need both, and we can go together, you and I, at our own pace."

So they started. Their way took them through the town of Vanity, where Faithful had been killed. But they passed through safely. Because of Faithful's death, many in that town now believed in the Kingdom of God.

"Take one of my crutches."

“That is where Giant Despair lives.”

8

The Delectable Mountains

The pilgrims then came to the River of God. Here they rested, eating fruit from the orchards and lying in the soft meadows, before setting out again.

Now as they went on, they came to a meadow on one side of the road. Through the meadow ran a path that went alongside the road. Here Great-heart stopped.

"Doubting Castle lies beyond that meadow," he said. "That is where Giant Despair lives."

On hearing the name, Christiana gasped. She had heard of her husband's trouble with that giant.

"It is time to end the reign of Despair," said Great-heart. "I have come this way for many years, but now I must deal with this evil giant. My Lord had bid me destroy both Despair and Doubting Castle."

"Let me go with you, Great-heart," said old Honest. "I have fought many a battle in my day. I can still wield a sword against wickedness."

Great-heart left Feeble-mind and Ready-to-halt to guard the women and children in the road. Then he and Honest went to the castle.

Great-heart strode to the doors of the courtyard and called to the giant.

"Who calls me?" roared Despair.

"It is I," said Great-heart, "the King's champion. I have come to destroy you and your castle! You will never again rob the Lord of His people!"

The heavy doors flew open. "I have come against angels!" said the giant. "Who are *you* to challenge me?" And he came out bellowing and swinging his club.

Great-heart and Honest had never fought so hard in their lives! The giant swung his heavy club with terrible strength. As the two men dodged his blows, the giant's club pounded deep into the earth, spewing out dirt and stones.

Suddenly out came another giant!

Suddenly from out of the castle came another giant, howling and cursing!

This was Despair's wife, Diffidence. She came at the two men with a great, curve-bladed knife.

Quickly old Honest met her charge. He ducked as she swung her knife. Then, with all his strength he lashed out, cutting her almost in two. Down she tumbled.

Now Honest turned to help his friend. Coming from behind, he hacked at the giant's legs. Howling, the giant fell to his knees.

Now Great-heart saw his chance. He leaped in and struck with the force of thunder. His sword came down on the giant's head, shattering his steel cap like glass.

Both giants lay dead.

The two men were panting and bleeding from their battle. They sat down to rest. Great-heart said, "Now we must tear this castle down to the ground. Despair and Diffidence will never again turn pilgrims out of the way."

It took seven days to destroy Doubting

Both giants lay dead.

Castle. Swinging great iron clubs, Great-heart and Honest smashed stones and splintered wooden beams. Whole walls crumbled. Tall towers fell.

In one courtyard were piles and piles of men's bones. These were all the pilgrims the giant had killed.

In the dungeons, Great-heart found a man and a girl chained to a wall. They were starved almost to death. Great-heart broke their chains.

"I am Despondency," said the man. "This is my daughter, Much-afraid. We cannot ever thank you enough, great one!"

"Come with us," said Great-heart.

When Christiana and the others saw Great-heart and Honest coming, they all began laughing and shouting. Then there was singing and dancing in the road! Even Ready-to-halt danced, hobbling about on just one crutch.

Mr. Despondency and his daughter were given food and drink. They wept for joy as

Great-heart broke their chains.

they ate, and strength and life came into them again.

Now that Despair and Doubting were gone, the pilgrims went more easily up the road. Even Feeble-mind felt stronger. And Ready-to-halt walked more steadily, his crutch only lightly touching the ground.

They came this way into the Delectable Mountains.

"Welcome, Mr. Great-heart and all of your friends," said the shepherds of these mountains. "The feeble and the weak, as well as the strong and the mighty, are always welcome here."

So the travelers rested there. Over the days that followed they were shown the things that were shown Christian and Hopeful before. And the shepherds showed them some new things.

They climbed a mountain called Innocent. There they saw a man in white clothes. Two other men called Prejudice and Ill-will were throwing dirt on the man in white. But the dirt

But the dirt would just fall off.

would just fall off, and the man's clothes were as white as ever.

"Who is this man?" asked Christiana.

One of the shepherds said, "This man is named Godly-man. His white garment shows that his life is innocent of all evil. The other two here are evil. They hate those who are innocent. But God Himself clothes the innocent, and He does not allow the dirt of sin to soil them."

Then they climbed another mountain called Charity. There a man sat cutting clothes from a bundle of cloth. Piles of these clothes lay all around him. Yet for all he cut, he did not run out of cloth.

"This man makes clothes for the poor," said a shepherd. "This is to show you that whoever gives to the poor will always have enough for himself."

The pilgrims stayed with the shepherds for several days. When it came time to leave, the shepherds said, "The way from here has many

Piles of clothes lay around him.

dangers. But they cannot conquer you, because your guide is Great-heart."

The road from the mountains went down through a thick forest. The pilgrims had not gone far when they came upon a man with a sword in his hand. He was tall and sinewy. Blood ran down his face and arms and down his hand onto his sword blade.

Great-heart gripped his sword. "Who are you?" he called.

The man was breathing hard. "I am called Valiant-for-truth," he said. "I am a pilgrim to the holy city. As I came this way, three men stopped me on the road. They said their names were Wildhead, Inconsiderate, and Pragmatic. They told me I was to choose to join them, to turn back, or to die."

"And you chose to fight?" said Great-heart.

"I did. We fought for hours. They just now ran off as they heard you coming. Though I bleed from their wounds, they bleed from many

"I am Valiant-for-truth."

more that I gave them."

Great-heart was beaming. "Now here is a fighting man!" he said. "Three against one!"

"Those odds are nothing to a man who has the truth on his side," said Valiant-for-truth. "As it is written, 'Even if a whole army surrounds me, I will not be afraid.' "*

"You have done well!" said Great-heart. "You have resisted unto blood, fighting against evil. Now come. Let us wash your wounds."

When this was done and they went on, Great-heart walked with Valiant-for-truth.

"Where are you from?" asked Great-heart.

"A place called Dark Land," said the other.

"Dark Land! That is an evil place. How did you come to leave there and travel this road?"

"One day a man named Tell-true came into my land and told us of a man named Christian who fought his way to the holy city. On hearing this, a burning desire grew in my heart to do the same."

---

*Psalm 27:3

Great-heart walked with Valiant-for-truth.

Then Great-heart said to Christiana, "You see? The story of your husband's faith has traveled all over this land."

"What!" said Valiant-for-truth, turning to Christiana. "You are Christian's wife?"

"Yes," she said. "And my sons and I have turned from unbelief to belief and now travel to the city, too."

"That day will be glad," said Valiant-for-truth, "when Christian's family comes to him in the city."

"Tell me," said Great-heart, "are you the only one from your land to come on this journey?"

"Yes," said Valiant-for-truth. "All the others, even my own family, reminded me of all the dangers. They told of Giant Despair and the rest. For fear of those things, no one would go with me. But I believed in the truth of Mr. Tell-true's story. And I believed that by faith I could overcome any danger on my journey."

"You are Christian's wife?"

Suddenly a black mist covered them.

9

Entering the Celestial City

When the travelers came to the place called the Enchanted Ground, Great-heart sent Valiant-for-truth to the rear of the company. "You guard from the rear," he said, "and I, from the front."

Since Christian and Hopeful had passed, this place had grown over with briars and thorns. Only here and there showed the enchanted flowers. Yet it was still a dangerous place. Great-heart and Valiant-for-truth went with their swords drawn.

And danger came quickly. As they walked, suddenly it was dark. A black mist covered them. Now the pilgrims could only follow Great-heart's voice. They held on to one another and groped along. Great-heart ahead and Valiant-for-truth behind spoke encouraging words to the other pilgrims. Then everyone began praying aloud to

God for deliverance from that evil darkness.

Soon a fresh wind began to blow. The mist began to clear. The wind continued to blow until the darkness had gone.

As the group drew near the end of the Enchanted Ground, they saw a man kneeling by the side of the road. He was praying. Then he got to his feet and started to go on.

"Hello, friend!" called Great-heart.

The man turned.

"I know this man!" said Honest. "He comes from a place near my home. His name is Stand-fast." He went up to the stranger.

"Well, Father Honest!" said the man. "Bless me! I did not know you were on this road."

"Tell us," said Valiant-for-truth. "Why were you praying just now?"

Stand-fast looked grave. "I have just passed through the Enchanted Ground as you have," he said. "It is a terrible place. But its danger does not compare to what I have just now faced. You

“Hello, friend!”

saw me praying for strength to resist temptation."

"What happened?" asked Honest.

"I had just passed out of the worst of the Enchanted Ground," said Stand-fast. "I was thinking of what a dangerous place that is, where a pilgrim may fall asleep and never wake again. I was thinking I had done well to pass through there, when a lady met me. She was tall and richly dressed. She said, 'Come with me. Be my husband and rule over me. I can give you riches and pleasures you have never dreamed of.'

"Now, I am very poor," continued Stand-fast. "And she was very beautiful. But I told her no. I would stay on the road, I said. She begged me to go with her, but I refused. She would not leave. So I knelt and prayed for deliverance from her. That is when you saw me."

"That lady," said Great-heart, "is a witch! She would have destroyed you.

"Her name is Madam Bubble," continued Great-heart. "She has been the death of many

“A tall lady met me.”

men who have followed her for her beauty and her wealth. She promises crowns and kingdoms but brings only death and destruction. She leads many to the gallows, many to hell. It is by her sorcery that this land behind us is enchanted."

"And where is she now?" asked Honest.

"After I prayed I looked up and she was gone," said Stand-fast. "I do not know where she went."

"She is not far," said Great-heart. "But prayer will keep her away. You are rightly named, my friend, for you stood fast when she came to you."

"Her beauty hides her evil well," said Stand-fast. "Where would she have led me if I had followed her?"

"Only God knows," said Great-heart, grimly. "It was she who led Judas to sell his Lord for thirty pieces of silver."

“I looked up, and she was gone.”

They came into the King's land.

10

Christiana in the Celestial City

Now came the end of the journey for the pilgrims.

They came into the King's land, full of beautiful meadows and orchards and vineyards.

The weary pilgrims now stood and stared in wonder at the beauty there. The sun was brighter than they had ever seen it, the sky bluer, the grass greener.

And as the travelers stood there, their weariness fell off them like a cloak. Feeble-mind threw his shoulders back like a prince. Ready-to-halt stood up straight and tall and threw away his crutch. The lines and creases were gone from old Honest's face.

Then a sound came to the pilgrims' ears. It was faint at first, as though from far away. It grew and grew.

From over the orchards and gardens, from over the river that lay ahead, from over the mountain past the river, from over the clouds at the top of the mountain—bells were ringing.

Now from out of the clouds on the mountain, down the mountain, across the river, and down the road came a rider on a horse. He flew like the wind.

The rider pulled up to the pilgrims. The horse pranced and blew steam from his nostrils. He was whiter than the whitest linen. On his forehead was a shining silver star.

The rider, too, was clothed in white. His blond hair streamed out over his shoulders. His beard flowed over his broad chest. At his side hung a great sword with a silver handle. He leaped from his horse and bowed to the pilgrims.

"I am the King's messenger," he said. "I have a letter from His Majesty."

He walked up to Christiana and bowed to her. "This is for you," he said.

Christiana's hand trembled as she took the letter. She opened it and read, "Welcome, Christiana, wife of Christian."

"This is for you."

"My Lord is calling for me!" cried Christiana. She clapped her hands for joy. "My journey is over. I will see my Lord, the King, and I will see my dear husband again!"

Now down the mountain came horses and chariots and crowds of people, singing and dancing. They stopped at the other side of the river, shouting and calling to Christiana.

The pilgrims went with Christiana up to the river. There she stopped to embrace her friends and to kiss them farewell.

"Do not cry," she said to her sons. "Soon I will see your father again, and you will come, too, when it is your time."

Now she started across the river. She did not stop or sink. She walked across the water. And her friends on this side and all the people on the other side cheered for her.

And she cried, "I am coming, my King!"

Christiana was taken up into the clouds and into the city. Now the rest of the pilgrims turned away from the river and walked back down to

"I am coming, my King!"

where they were staying in the gardens.

"The Lord will call each of you in your turn," said Great-heart. "Enjoy yourselves here in His gardens while you wait for Him."

This they did. And they were not alone. There were many gardeners there, tending the King's fruit trees and gardens.

And children came daily to the gardens from the city, to gather flowers and spices for the King's palace. There were never any tears or quarreling among these children, only laughter and singing. Christiana's sons played with the children in the gardens. The heavenly children taught the boys their songs and games.

And when the children wanted to dance, they would come streaming up to Great-heart, and he would play the pipes for them.

The messenger came next for Mr. Ready-to-halt. "The King would like you to dine with Him in His palace," said the messenger.

Ready-to-halt called his friends together. "I am to dine with the King tonight in His palace,"

Christiana was taken into the city.

he said. "And soon, I know, all of you will be with me there. And thank you, Sir Great-heart, for bringing me safely here. Without you I would have been lost."

And he walked, without his crutches, across the river.

Soon the messenger came for Feeble-mind. "I have come to tell you that your Master wants you," said the messenger. "Now you will see His face in brightness."

Feeble-mind said to his friends, "Now I will leave my feeble mind behind me. I have no need for weakness where I am going."

And as his friends cheered him, he walked boldly across the river shouting, "My faith holds out to the end!"

Now the messenger came back for Mr. Despondency. "Trembling man," said the messenger, "the King summons you. Shout for joy, because He has delivered you from all Doubt."

He walked boldly across the river.

As Despondency crossed the river he shouted, "Farewell, night! Welcome day!" His daughter went with him, and they walked up the mountain.

The rest were called for, one by one.

Honest said, "Though I go, I have nothing to leave behind. I take my honesty with me."

"And I," said Valiant-for-truth, "carry my battle scars with me. Yet I leave my sword for any who has the courage and skill to use it."

When the last had gone over, Great-heart stood alone on the other side of the river. Now he shouted for joy.

"Hail, Lord!" he cried. "May all Your people praise You forever! Now I return, to bring more pilgrims to You."

And he turned and walked back down the road, tightening his sword belt.